Young Werewolf

illustrated by David Roberts

Young Werewolf

CORNELIA FUNKE

Barrington Stoke

For Robin, from Cornelia

Published in Germany as *Kleiner Werwolf* by
Cecilie Dressler Verlag GmbH, Hamburg, 2002

First published in 2013 in Great Britain by
Barrington Stoke Ltd
18 Walker Street, Edinburgh, EH3 7LP

www.barringtonstoke.co.uk

Text © 2002 Cornelia Funke
Illustrations © David Roberts
Translated from the German by Oliver Latsch

ISBN: 978-1-78112-268-6

Printed in China by Leo

CONTENTS

1. AN EERIE ENCOUNTER

It happened on a Sunday evening in October.

A horrid evening.

Matt and Lisa had gone to the cinema. When they stepped out onto the street after the film, it was already dark. Matt didn't like the dark. If it was up to him, he would have banned the night a long time ago. The night and the moon and everything else that went with it.

A cold, wet wind blew into Matt and Lisa's faces. It whipped up the fallen leaves. People turned up their collars as they rushed home. Dogs growled at each other. And above them all, the moon hung milky white between the clouds.

"What a stupid film," Lisa said. "Totally stupid."

Without another word she started towards home. She took such long strides that Matt had trouble keeping up, as usual. Lisa was a head taller than Matt, and she was his very best friend.

"I didn't think the film was that bad," Matt said.

"You don't say," Lisa mocked.

Matt and Lisa did not like the same films. Lisa liked anything with animals. Matt liked space stories. Lisa liked films where everyone was terribly nice to each other. Matt liked ones crammed with baddies. But they both enjoyed arguing about films, much more than they enjoyed the films themselves.

They turned into the small path that led to the railway underpass. Their breath hung in the air like white smoke.

"Brrr!" Lisa's face screwed up. "I hate going through here. It smells and it's creepy."

"Oh, come on," Matt said. After he had watched a film, he always felt a little braver than usual.

The underpass gaped like a black mouth. It did not look very welcoming at all, but it was the shortest way home.

Lisa took Matt's hand. "Yuck!" she said. "It smells worse than usual today, doesn't it? And there's something different about the smell ..." Her steps made eerie echoes in the darkness, and her voice sounded strange and hollow. "Hello?" she called. "Is anybody there?"

"Lisa, stop that!" Matt said. He felt his way along the cold, wet tunnel wall. In his

3

imagination, he was Commander Matt and he had landed on an unexplored planet. But the darkness made his heart race, even as Commander Matt.

A train thundered above their heads. Then the silence returned.

"Matt!" Lisa whispered. "Matt, look over there."

"Stop the stupid jokes!" Matt growled back.

But Lisa wasn't joking.

The light of a street lamp glowed at the other end of the tunnel. And right there, just one step from the exit, Matt saw a dark shape.

It wasn't human. A fox, perhaps? No ... a dog.

"Great," said Matt. "You like dogs, don't you?"

Matt didn't like dogs at all. Not one bit.

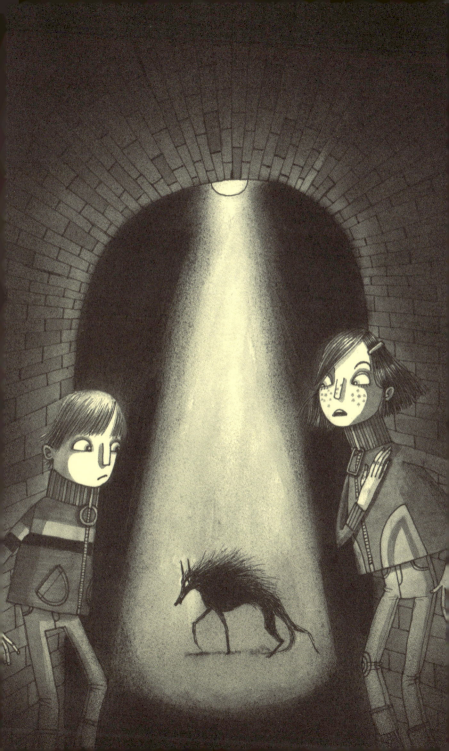

"I don't like that one," Lisa whispered. "It looks scary. Hadn't we better turn back?"

Matt shook his head. Nonsense! Turn back because of a dog? He could imagine what his big brother would have to say about that. He took a deep breath and walked towards the dark shape.

As Matt got nearer, the dog lifted its head and sniffed. Its eyes were bright yellow, like glowing amber. Its tail was firmly tucked between its legs.

Matt squeezed against the tunnel wall. The more distance he could put between that pointed muzzle and himself, the better.

"It's got yellow eyes!" Lisa hissed. "No dog has yellow eyes." She tried to pull Matt away by his arm. "Get away! That's a wolf. A real wolf!"

"Rubbish!" Matt pushed himself further along the tunnel wall. This was ridiculous. Who ever heard of a wolf in the middle of the city?

The dog lifted its head and followed him with its eyes. They glowed in the darkness like golden fires.

Matt was just about to push past when his foot hit an empty drink can. With a great deal of noise, it rolled against the dog's paws.

Matt gave a start.

Lisa screamed.

And the dog snapped at Matt's hand.

It was as quick as lightning. So quick that it hardly hurt.

Then the dog made a leap and vanished into the darkness.

"He bit you!" Lisa screamed. "Oh no, he bit you! Does it hurt?"

"No," Matt muttered. He stared at the black tunnel wall. Best not to look at his hand.

"Come on!" Lisa said. She pulled Matt out of the tunnel and over to a street light.

Matt screwed his eyes shut and held out his hand. It felt very hot. Hot and throbbing.

"You were lucky!" Lisa said. "It doesn't look that bad."

"Really?" Matt still didn't dare to look at his hand. He was sure it was an awful mess. "Isn't it, like, all torn up and stuff?" he asked.

"Not at all!" Lisa giggled. "It's just a scratch."

Matt opened his eyes. "I can't stand seeing blood. It makes me feel all weird."

"Who'd have thought it?" Lisa said. She pulled a tissue from her jacket pocket and wrapped it round his hand. "What about those films you always drag me to? They're full of blood!"

"Films are different," Matt said.

On shaky legs, Matt followed Lisa across the street and past the shops that were closing for the night. At last, they reached the building where both of them lived. Matt was on the ground floor, Lisa right at the top.

"OK, then." Lisa pushed the door open. "Go and see a doctor tomorrow, yeah? In case of rabies."

"Yeah, yeah!" Matt watched as she skipped up the stairs on her long legs. Then he hid his hand in his jacket pocket and pressed the doorbell.

2. FUR AND CLAWS

Matt's parents and his big brother Paul were already sitting at the dinner table.

"So?" Paul asked. "How was the film?"

"Great!" Matt hid his hand under the table, but it was hard to use a knife and fork with one hand.

"What happened to your hand?" Matt's mum reached across, but Matt made his hand vanish under the table again. If his mother saw the bite she would drag him straight to a doctor. Matt liked doctors even less than dogs. And the only things worse than doctors were Biology teachers ... but that was a different story.

"We have a maths test tomorrow," he said. It was a white lie, but it was sure to distract his parents.

"Oh dear!" said his mum.

"Have you studied enough?" his dad asked. "Perhaps you should sit down with your brother for an hour after dinner."

Paul was a maths whizz. He sat opposite Matt as smug as a king on his throne, two years older, a foot taller and unfazed by any subject the teachers could throw at him.

"How about it, little brother?" he asked. "Need me to tutor you some more?"

"Nope, it's just a little test," Matt answered, as he stuffed two slices of salami into his mouth. "I can do it myself." He sniffed. "Did you buy that smelly cheese again, Mum? Yuck."

"Sorry?" His mother looked at him in surprise. "I made sure to leave it in the fridge. You can't smell it from here, can you?"

"In the fridge?" Matt mumbled. There was a strong smell of cheese. Weird.

"If anything smells, mate, it's you," Paul said. "Your breath stinks like Mr Clapper's pitbull's. What did you do? Eat a tin of dog food?"

At the mention of 'dog', Matt spluttered and had a coughing fit.

"Goodness!" His mother turned up her nose. "Paul's right. Your breath smells awful. Go and brush your teeth."

"I'm going!" Matt got up. His skin was itching terribly. He saw yellow flashes in front of his eyes. He felt very strange. Was this how rabies started?

He stumbled into the bathroom. Normally he fumbled for ages in the dark for the light switch, but now he could see it quite clearly. Weird. He closed the door without switching on the light. He could still see everything perfectly. He could even read the label on Paul's spot cream. The darkness was little more than a grey haze.

'Weird,' Matt thought again. He rubbed his itchy face. His cheeks felt like his father's when he needed a shave.

Then he looked in the mirror – and jumped back so fast in shock that he nearly ended up in the bath.

Yellow eyes.

Yellow eyes stared back at him from the mirror.

And those eyes were part of a horrid, hairy, monster face.

Matt looked at his sore hand. It was hairy like a guinea pig's, with little pointy claws where his nails used to be. The other hand looked totally normal. He peered under his T-shirt. Not a single hair. Well, that was something at least.

With shaky knees, Matt pushed himself up from the rim of the bath and stood in front of the mirror again.

The only thing that hadn't changed was his nose. His eyebrows were bushier. His cheeks and chin were covered in fine grey hairs. And as he tried a smile, two pointy fangs pushed out over his lower lip.

The eyes were the worst. Wild, yellow and glowing.

Somebody knocked on the bathroom door.

"Matthew?" It was his mother. She was the only one who called him that. "What have you

been doing in there all this time?" she asked. "Your dad and I have to use the bathroom. We're going out tonight."

"I'll be out in a second," Matt tried to say, but it came out as a growl.

"Goodness! Have you caught a cold?" his mother asked. "Your voice sounds terrible."

"I just choked on something," Matt growled. His yellow eyes glowed in the darkness.

"Heavens! Choked on what? You sound like a wild animal!" his mother said. "Could you come out now?"

"I'm on the loo!" Matt barked back. He pulled the flush.

"All right then. But hurry up!" Her steps receded down the hallway.

Matt stared at his reflection in the mirror. He wasn't sure whether he should laugh or cry. 'I have to talk to Lisa,' he thought. 'But first, I have to get to my room without anyone seeing me.'

He pressed his ear against the bathroom door.

His hearing was excellent now – much better than before.

"I think I'll have to take Matthew to the doctor tomorrow!" he heard his mother say in the kitchen. Her voice was so clear. He could even hear her dress swish as she sat down.

"You always run straight to the doctor with him," his father grumbled. "You're spoiling him."

"But his voice!" his mum said. "You should have heard his voice. It was spooky."

His father laughed. "It's a bit early for his voice to break, isn't it?"

"Maybe he's pretending to be sick so he can get out of the maths test tomorrow," Paul suggested.

So Paul was still in the kitchen too.

Matt opened the bathroom door a crack. He carefully pushed his shaggy head through and vanished round the corner into his room.

Closed the door.

Locked it.

Safety.

"Matthew?" his mum called from the kitchen. "Shall I make you a hot drink?"

"No!" Matt called back.

"Wow, he does sound kind of bad," Paul said.

Matt opened the window as fast as he could. The cold air cooled his furry face. Outside, Lisa's message tube hung on a washing line. But just as Matt was about to pull it into the room he saw someone on the other side of the street. It was Mrs Brewer, of all people. She was the nosiest person on earth. If she saw Matt like this, the fire brigade would be knocking down the door within ten minutes, searching for a monster.

But after Mrs Brewer had peered into a few windows, she crossed the street and vanished into the building. She lived on the third floor, beneath Lisa's family.

For a few moments the street was deserted. Only a lonely cat crept around the parked cars. The cat hissed when she saw Matt and then vanished under one of the cars. Matt pulled the tube in through the window and ducked out of sight again.

The tube had been Lisa's idea. It was for secret messages, or for when neither of them could sleep. It was a cardboard postage tube, wrapped in plastic so it wouldn't get wet. It hung out of Lisa's window on a washing line. There was a bell at Lisa's end of the line, so she could hear when Matt put something into the tube. If Lisa wanted to send something, she just let it drop down and bang against Matt's window.

Matt found it easy to open the tube with his new claws. He dropped a red marble into it. Lisa would know what that meant. *Urgent meeting in the secret hideout – red alert!*

When Matt pushed the tube out of the window he could hear the bell ring up at Lisa's. He hoped she was in her room. She was normally in her room around this time. *Please, please, please let her be there!*

He was in luck, for the first time on this bad-luck Sunday. The tube lurched upwards. Matt was so relieved that he almost forgot to duck under the windowsill again.

"We're leaving!" his mum called from outside his room.

"Have fun!" Matt called back.

"Good grief!" he heard his father say. "That boy does sound awful!"

The front door banged shut and Paul came down the hallway and went into his room. Matt knew that he would plant himself in front of his computer and wouldn't be seen or heard for the rest of the evening.

Matt waited for the tube for what seemed like an eternity. When at last it came down again there were two red marbles inside. That meant *I'm coming!*

Matt pressed his shaggy forehead to his knees and sighed. 'Lisa will know what to do,' he thought. 'She'll come up with something.' Now Matt just had to figure out how to get upstairs without ending up in a zoo. His and Lisa's secret hideout was in the attic of the building.

Matt tried to think. It wasn't easy – a thousand sounds filled his ears, a thousand smells crept into his nose. It was enough to drive you crazy. No human could think like that. But was Matt still a human?

'Maybe I should just go to bed and pull the blanket over my head,' Matt thought. 'Hang on – the bed!' Yes, that could work. He pulled off the sheet and put it over his head. Better to look like a ghost than a monster. He cut two holes for his eyes and crept out of the room in disguise.

3. MR CLAPPER'S PITBULL

There was no reaction from Paul when Matt opened the front door. The light in the hall was off, but now to Matt's eyes there was no darkness. That was a good thing – a very good thing. He sneaked up the stairs without a sound.

Second floor.

Third floor.

But then Mr Clapper came out of his flat with his pitbull, Nero.

Whenever Matt heard Nero panting down the stairs, he would hide behind the door.

Normally. But tonight nothing was normal. Mr Clapper's pitbull was just a few steps away from him, but Matt was not afraid.

"Aaah!" Mr Clapper screamed. "Attack, Nero, go!"

Mrs Brewer put her head around her door, saw a ghost and locked the door again quick smart.

Mr Clapper dropped Nero's lead. Nero bared his teeth, pricked his ears and jumped at Matt. Any other day, Matt would have tumbled backwards down the stairs. But not today. Today his back arched and his upper lip jerked upward. "Rrrrrrr!" he growled, from the depths of his chest. "Raaaargggh!" He bared his teeth and the hairs on his back stood up. His claws tore through the bed sheet.

The pitbull retreated with a loud whine. He tried to hide behind Mr Clapper, who was

shaking and leaning against the door of his flat with his hands pressed over his eyes.

Matt growled one last time. Then he stumbled past Mr Clapper and his dog and raced up the stairs to the fourth floor, where he vanished through the attic door.

"H-h-help," he heard Mr Clapper squeal in a thin voice. "H-h-help!"

Matt ran over to a huge wardrobe that stood in the darkest corner of the attic. He tore the door open and crawled past old winter coats and discarded dresses. Then he pushed his way through to the back.

And there it was – Matt and Lisa's secret hideout. It smelled of mice and mothballs, old pizza and Lisa's shampoo.

"At last!" Lisa said. She was sitting on an old broken sofa, with her feet on a small, wobbly table. "What's with the disguise?" she asked.

"Hello!" Matt said. He was shaking all over. "Could you switch off the light, please?"

"Switch *off* the light? Are you crazy? Usually it can't be too bright for you." Lisa lifted her feet off the table and got up. "So ... why the red alert? And what's with your voice? You sound like Frankenstein's Monster or something."

"Something terrible has happened," Matt told her. "Really terrible. But don't be scared, OK?"

He took a deep breath and pulled the bed sheet off his head.

Lisa squealed like a little pig.

She grabbed an iron candlestick, jumped on the sofa and screamed some more.

That was the last straw for Matt. It was all just too much. First that yellow-eyed dog bit him and turned him into a monster. Then Mr

Clapper's pitbull attacked him. And now his very best friend was screaming her head off at the sight of him. He collapsed on the carpet and started to sob. The tears ran down his hairy cheeks and dripped onto the furry paw that had once been his hand.

Lisa fell silent. Silent as the grave.

"I thought you would help me!" Matt snivelled. "I thought, 'Lisa will think of something.' But you're just standing there and screaming like a banshee."

After a moment, Lisa climbed down from the sofa. She put the candlestick back on the table and sat down in front of him.

"Matt?" she asked quietly.

"What?" With his normal hand Matt rubbed the tears from his fur.

"It's really you." Lisa sounded like she couldn't believe it.

"Of course it's me," Matt growled. "Who else would it be? An alien? Or what?"

Lisa reached out her hand and stroked his furry cheek. Then, all of a sudden, she started to giggle.

"That's amazing," she said. "It's like in the film, right?"

"I don't think it's amazing at all," Matt grumbled.

"Have your parents seen you like this?" Lisa asked.

"Are you crazy? Nobody's seen me like this. That's why I was under the bed sheet. Mrs Brewer poked her nose into the hall when I passed, of course. Now she thinks our building is haunted. Mr Clapper nearly had a heart attack. And his dog ..." At last, Matt had to smile. "His dog actually ran away from me."

"Clapper's pitbull?" Lisa asked, amazed. "That monster ran away from you?"

Matt nodded. That had felt good. But he also felt uneasy about what had happened in the hall. He had been more afraid of himself than of Mr Clapper's pitbull.

"Do you think I have rabies, Lisa?" he asked.

"Of course not!" Lisa took his sore hand, which was now a paw. She looked into his hairy face. "I think you're a werewolf."

"A what?" Matt asked, confused.

"A werewolf," Lisa repeated. "I saw a film about them once. It was horrible. This guy got bitten by a wolf and after that he turned into a wolf a little bit more every night." Lisa looked at Matt. "You already look a bit like a wolf."

"A little bit more every night?" Matt looked at his claws. "You think this will get worse?"

Lisa shrugged. "That's what happened in the film."

"And then?" Matt asked. "What happened then? In the film?"

"I don't know," Lisa said. But she said it a little too fast. And she also licked her lips. She always did that when she was lying.

"What happened then, Lisa?" Matt asked again.

"What? Oh, he always went back to normal in the morning," Lisa said. "But I don't remember any more." And she licked her lips again.

"*Went back to normal*," Matt muttered.

"Yes. He was only a wolf when it was dark."

"Right." Matt nodded. "Well, that wouldn't be too bad. I can't go to school like this, can I?"

"It would make an interesting change," Lisa giggled. "You could give our stupid Biology teacher a real fright!"

"Tempting," Matt said. "Very tempting."

Lisa stroked his paw to comfort him. "I'll think of something," she said. "I always think of something. You know that."

"I do," said Matt.

But this time he wasn't so sure.

4. TWO DAYS TO THE FULL MOON

The next day it was all gone – the fur on Matt's face, the claws, the bushy eyebrows and the rough voice. There was just the gash left on his hand, but Matt could still hear and smell much better than before.

At breakfast time, his dad's aftershave stung his nose. As he put on his jacket he could hear people upstairs talking about the ghost Mr Clapper and Mrs Brewer had seen in the hall. *The ghost that growled.* Matt couldn't help smiling.

"What are you grinning about?" his mum asked. She put his sandwich in his school bag. Salami. His lucky day!

"Mrs Brewer called the fire brigade again yesterday," his mum went on. "Just imagine! This time she says she saw a ghost."

"And then what?" Matt asked. "What happened?" His hand was itchy. He had put a huge plaster on it.

"The fire brigade refused to come," his mum said. Then she took hold of Matt's cheeks and turned his face towards her. "That's odd," she said. "Your voice is back to normal, but your eyes are strange. Really yellow."

"Yeah right, Mum!" Matt said and he turned his head away again.

His mum kissed his cheek. Then she jumped back. "Matthew!" she cried. "You have stubble! Paul! Come and feel this."

"Wow!" said Paul. "You need a shave, little brother!"

"I must be an early developer," Matt said.

Paul looked at Matt with envy. He still didn't have a single hair on his own face, even though he stood in front of the bathroom mirror on the lookout every morning.

Matt thanked his lucky stars when, at that very moment, Lisa rang the doorbell.

"You look pretty normal," Lisa said, as she and Matt walked down the street. "It's just your eyes …"

"I know," said Matt. "I'll have to buy sunglasses. Have you thought of anything yet?"

Lisa chuckled. "Get yourself a good razor!"

"Ha, ha," Matt grumbled.

He was feeling very, very weird. He was getting used to hearing flies sneeze and smelling what people had eaten for breakfast.

But now there was something else – something that frightened him.

"Look!" Lisa stopped in front of the pet shop they passed every morning. "They have new guinea pigs. Aren't they cute?"

"Mmm!" Matt muttered. "They look nice and juicy."

Lisa looked at him in horror. "What did you say?"

"That just slipped out," Matt said. He licked his lips and his stomach grumbled. "Lisa, I'm not going to school today," he said.

"What?" Lisa looked at him in surprise.

A man with a huge German Shepherd dog passed by. The dog growled. Matt bared his teeth and growled back. The dog nearly jumped into the road. Then it dragged its owner away, its tail between its legs.

Lisa looked at Matt with concern.

"You see?" he asked.

She nodded. "You should see a doctor."

"I will," Matt promised. "But first I have to find out more about this werewolf thing. And I won't be able to do that at school."

Lisa shook her head. "No, definitely not," she said. "I suggest we get ourselves some books."

* * *

That early in the morning they were the only two visitors in the library.

Matt found seven books about werewolves in the catalogue on the computer. One was a picture book and one was a pop-up book about monsters. Two more were about people who just thought they were werewolves. The other three were in the grown-up section.

"Let's go," Lisa said.

"That's the grown-up section!" the librarian called as they sneaked past her.

"We know!" Lisa called back.

The librarian gave them a grouchy look and went back to chewing her pencil.

All three books were on the shelf. They looked quite old. Lisa took them down and pulled Matt over to a table where the librarian couldn't see them. Then she opened the first book. Lisa read faster than Matt could turn the pages. She frowned as she leaned over the yellow pages. It was very quiet. Matt could hear the librarian biting her nails.

"Here's something," Lisa whispered. "Listen! 'Many cultures have stories about people who turn into wolves after being bitten by a wolf. Usually the first effect the victim feels is a slight itching of the skin, very soon followed by increased hair growth. The eyes turn yellow and the sense of smell and hearing improve as the nature of the wolf takes over the victim.'"

Matt collapsed in his chair. "Sounds horrible," he whispered.

"'On the following nights,'" Lisa read on, "'the disease progresses. The changes happen steadily until the next full moon, when the victim turns into a werewolf and will never again shed his wolf-like features.'"

"The next full moon?" Matt asked. "When is that?"

Lisa shrugged. "Dunno."

"And?" Matt shifted in his chair, worried. "Does it say what you can do to stop it?"

Lisa shook her head, closed the book and opened the next one.

Matt rubbed his sore hand. The librarian peered over the shelf at them and he bared his teeth at her.

"Stop that!" Lisa hissed. "Here's something else. 'As soon as the victim notices the first signs of change he should stop eating any meat, avoid any contact with dogs and lock himself up at night, so that he may not get outside. It is only out of doors that the nature of the wolf can take full hold of him. Nothing strikes so much fear into humans as the wolf, even though it is a shy and timid animal and not at all vicious. All through history humans have shown hatred and anger towards wolf-men. They have hunted them down and killed them whenever they could.'"

"*Hunted them down*," Matt whispered. "Help! Is there anything else?"

Lisa shook her head and reached for the third book.

"Here!" she called. "This could be important. It says something about charms that can drive out the wolf. Wait. It says that charms of this type were even put into graves." Lisa rubbed her earlobes. "They should have these things in the museum, right?"

Matt shook his head. "What museum?"

"How about the Natural History Museum?" Lisa said. "I …"

"Will you look at that!" a voice said behind them. "Who do we have here?"

Lisa and Matt did not have to turn around to know who was standing behind them.

"Morning, Sir." Lisa put her hand over what she had been reading. "What are you doing here?"

"Oh, no," the voice said. "The real question is what are *you* two doing here?"

It was Mr Foulweather, Biology teacher.

Special interest – the destruction of students' souls.

Favourite hobby – the torture of children.

Worse than wolves, dogs, dentists and all other fearsome creatures combined.

Much worse.

"Interesting …" Mr Foulweather said and he reached with his long fingers for the book in front of Lisa. "'Mysterious creatures – Vampires, Ghosts, Werewolves.' Well, well, well. An interesting subject. But –" He looked at his watch. "Shouldn't you be working on your English essays right now?"

"We, um, got a pass," Matt lied. "For a project."

"Indeed?" Mr Foulweather said. "And for what subject, if I may ask? This topic here seems to fall in my area of expertise." He stared at Matt's face. "But I didn't give you a pass."

Matt felt his upper lip begin to twitch. A growl started to grow in his chest. He pressed his hand in front of his mouth. But he chose the wrong one.

"Will you look at that!" Mr Foulweather cried. "What bit you? Fascinating." He put his hand under Matt's chin and looked into his eyes.

Matt nearly snapped at Mr Foulweather's hand. Lisa gave him a shove with her knee just in time.

"Your eyes are an odd colour," Mr Foulweather said. He stroked along Matt's cheek with a long, bony finger. "And you have a lot of stubble for your age."

"He drank a cure for baldness," Lisa jumped in. "His father's. That's what gave him the yellow eyes."

"Is that so?" Mr Foulweather smiled. "Well, we'll see each other later. Fourth period, yes?"

The two of them nodded.

"Good luck with your essay," the teacher said. "And by the way, did you know that the next full moon is in two nights? See you later."

Mr Foulweather vanished between the shelves.

"Two nights," Lisa whispered.

"Why did he say that?" Matt muttered. But then he pricked his ears and put his fingers to his lips. "The creep is still here," he whispered. "I can hear him breathing. Let's talk about something else."

Lisa nodded and began to chat as she put the books back on the shelf. Matt could hear Mr Foulweather sneak away. 'You're not quiet enough for wolf ears, creep,' he thought.

By the time Matt and Lisa got to the librarian's desk, Mr Foulweather was nowhere to be seen. But Matt could hear him scratching himself in the Arts and Crafts section. What was the creep up to?

"We want to check out this book," Lisa told the librarian.

"But that's a grown-up book," the librarian replied. She smelled of lavender soap, ink and mouth-wash.

Matt just stared at her with his yellow eyes.

The librarian plucked nervously at her frilly blouse. "Fine, if that's what you're interested in," she said at last. "Your library card, please."

Matt really would have to get those sunglasses.

5. A HELPER

Foulweather followed them. All the way from the library to the school.

"What does he want?" Matt growled. He pulled his sandwich from his bag and was about to take a bite when Lisa took it out of his hand.

"Salami," she said. "That's not good for you. Here, have mine."

"Cheese!" Matt groaned. "Yuck. Wolves don't eat cheese."

"Exactly," Lisa replied. She bit into Matt's salami sandwich.

"Why don't we go straight to the museum?" Matt asked.

"With Foulweather on our tail? Are you crazy?" Lisa shook her head. "No, I have a much better idea. We'll go to the museum while he's teaching our class."

Matt stared at her, impressed. "Cheeky!"

"Yes, but first I'll take you to the doctor," Lisa said. "We can do that before Maths. After all, even werewolves can die of rabies, right?"

* * *

But Mr Foulweather spoiled their plan. When Lisa and Matt (now vaccinated against rabies) returned to school in time for their Maths lesson, Mrs Ruskin was waiting for them by the classroom door. She was their form teacher and she was wearing her best 'what-have-you-done-now' face.

"Mr Foulweather tells me that you were in the library instead of class this morning," she said.

"Jerk!" Matt growled.

"Pardon me?" Mrs Ruskin gave Matt a stern glare. But she didn't look stern for long – her eyes opened wide in surprise. "You've got yellow eyes, Matt Smith," she said.

"Yes, he has," Lisa said. She looked around. "Can we talk in private?"

Matt looked at her in shock. Had she gone crazy?

"We need her help," Lisa hissed in his ear. "Let me handle this, OK?"

"What do you mean, in private?" Mrs Ruskin asked. She still sounded cross.

Lisa lowered her voice. "I mean somewhere Mr Foulweather can't hear us. This is mega-secret."

"So it seems," Mrs Ruskin muttered.

She thought about it for a moment and then pulled them into the Chemistry lab. Matt's wolf nose noted at least twenty unpleasant smells.

Mrs Ruskin sat on the desk. "Let's hear it, then," she said. She rubbed her nose.

"Matt is a werewolf," Lisa said. "Since yesterday."

"Pardon?" Mrs Ruskin said. Then she sneezed so hard that her hairdo wobbled. Mrs Ruskin always had very fancy hairdos. "What did you say?"

"A wolf bit him," Lisa explained. "Last night, on the way back from the cinema. And since then he's turned into a werewolf."

Mrs Ruskin sneezed again, three times in a row. "Sorry," she snuffled. "I'm allergic to dogs. There must be a dog here somewhere ..." She looked around.

"That's what I'm saying!" Lisa shouted. "It's Matt. You're sneezing because of Matt. Because he's a wolf."

Mrs Ruskin leaned against the desk and closed her eyes. Then she opened them again and sneezed another three times.

"Proof," she said. "I want proof. Apart from the sneezing, I mean!"

"Feel my cheeks!" Matt said.

Mrs Ruskin did as he told her. "Amazing!" she said. "Facial hair! You have a distinct growth of facial hair. And your eyes ..."

Matt held out his sore hand. "See?"

There were hairs growing all round the bite marks – fine grey hairs. "We've just been to the doctor," Matt said. "He suspected something was up. Lisa had to talk nineteen to the dozen to persuade him not to keep me in."

"Last night Matt had claws," Lisa added. "And his face felt fluffy like a guinea pig's."

Mrs Ruskin sneezed again – six times.

"That's incredible," she said. "I heard about things like that when I was at university. But ... no." She shook her head. "I'm sorry. I just can't believe it."

"But you have to believe us!" Lisa shouted.

Matt said nothing. He lifted his nose and sniffed. Mrs Ruskin looked at him in surprise. "What are you doing, Matt?" she asked.

"What if I told you what you had for breakfast?" Matt said. "Would that be proof?"

Mrs Ruskin looked at him for a long moment. "Maybe. Let's hear it."

"Apricot jam," Matt began. "Toast, eggs, tea with lemon. And you used a lot of hairspray, not the same brand my mother uses. And that small stain there on your skirt ..." Matt sniffed again. "That was sausage, but you washed it out with washing-up liquid."

Mrs Ruskin looked down at her skirt – and sneezed three times.

"That's all true!" She sniffed. She rubbed her nose with a flowery hankie for quite a while. Matt kept his eyes firmly on her. "And if I believed you?" she said at last. "What then?"

"Do you know when the next full moon is?" Matt asked.

"Day after tomorrow," Mrs Ruskin said. "Well, the night of the day after tomorrow. Why?"

"At the next full moon Matt will turn into a wolf for ever!" Lisa told her.

"Oh my goodness!" Mrs Ruskin gasped.

Matt looked at her with his yellow eyes.

"No, no, no!" Mrs Ruskin said. She patted her hair into place. "We can't let that happen. I mean, no one likes wolves, do they? I can't bear to think about what they might do to you, Matt. Oh, my goodness!" She closed her eyes. "What are we going to do?"

"We have to get to the Natural History Museum," Lisa said. "People used to have charms for werewolf magic. We read that in the library."

"When Mr Foulweather caught you skipping school." Mrs Ruskin shook her head. "Bad luck! Yes, my dear colleague Mr Foulweather has always been very interested in werewolves, vampires and the like. In the staffroom we call him Dracula. His big dream is to find scientific evidence for the existence of such creatures. And what could be better than to catch a live werewolf? This is quite a pickle!" Mrs Ruskin chewed her lower lip. "I will have to help you. Let's meet this afternoon at 4.30 in front of the museum. It closes early today, but I know one of the scientists there. I will ask him to lend me one of the werewolf charms to show my class – if they have one. And then we'll put it on Matt. What do you think?"

"Wonderful!" Lisa said.

Matt nodded and then stiffened as he heard a new sound.

"What is it?" Lisa whispered.

Matt ran to the door and tore it open.

There was nobody outside. But a smell lingered in the air. A smell he'd met before. Somewhere a door closed.

"Foulweather!" Matt said. "Crisps, cigarettes, sweaty socks – that's his smell."

"Then he must have heard us talking about the museum," Lisa groaned.

"Doesn't matter," Mrs Ruskin said. "What's he going to do? He's welcome to creep after us if he wants to."

"But what if it's dark when we come out of the museum?" Matt asked. "What if he sees me change?"

"He won't," Mrs Ruskin said. "We'll hurry. It won't get dark before six. I'll take you home in my car well before then."

"OK," Matt said.

But he was still a little afraid.

6. THE CHARM

There was a strong wind blowing that afternoon and dark rain clouds were piling up in the sky. When Matt and Lisa headed to the museum the sky was almost pitch black, despite the fact that it was only 4.30 p.m.

Matt's skin tingled like crazy. But that wasn't the worst of it. His stomach started rumbling every time he saw a small dog. He caught himself snapping at flies. He gave a sparrow such a longing look that Lisa had to pull him away. It was horrible. His ears hurt from the traffic noise and the fumes from the cars almost choked him. No, it wasn't easy being a wolf in a big city.

On the other hand, being a wolf had some good sides. Matt normally had trouble keeping up with Lisa and her long legs. Now Lisa was the one who was out of breath as they climbed the stairs to the museum. Matt's legs moved with almost no effort, fast and light.

"Why are you running like that?" Lisa panted. "Now we'll be waiting outside the door for ages."

"Now you can see what it's like for me!" Matt said. "And anyway, it's not my fault."

Matt's voice already sounded a little rougher and deeper than usual. He hopped from one foot to the other and sniffed the air. They hadn't spotted Mr Foulweather on the way to the museum. But now his scent was very strong in Matt's nose. It was as obvious as a wrong note in a song.

"He's here," Matt growled. He took another deep sniff through his nose. "Foulweather is here."

"Where?" Lisa looked around, alarmed. Countless people rushed past the bottom of the steps, vanished into cafés or shops, reappeared, crossed the wide street on which the cars were crawling past. Spotting anyone in this bustle would be impossible.

"I can smell him," Matt insisted.

Then they heard somebody call. "Hello-o! Hello-o-o!" Mrs Ruskin came panting up the stairs. "I have good news – they do have a charm here!" she said. "Several of them! Isn't that wonderful?"

Mrs Ruskin walked up to the large door and pressed the bell. Half a lifetime later a skinny man with a wisp of a beard opened it and peered out. "My dear Balty!" Mrs Ruskin greeted him. "I would like you to meet two very interesting students of mine. This is Matthew Smith." She sneezed twice. "And Lisa Harman. This is Dr Balthazar Squint. He is an important expert on early history."

Dr Squint's face broke into a shy smile. "Good afternoon," he said. "Please come in. We do indeed have some objects you might find interesting, my dear Amelia. Shall I take you to the charms right away?"

"Oh yes, please," said Matt. His stomach was rumbling louder and louder and he could already feel the tiny claws sprouting from his sore hand. He stuffed his hand in his pocket.

Dr Squint led them upstairs and through gloomy hall after gloomy hall. Scary masks stared down at them and there were strange wooden figures and poles with ugly carved faces on them.

"These are so spooky in the dark," Lisa whispered. "Don't you think?"

But Matt shook his head. To his wolf eyes the museum was as bright as day and the strange figures seemed oddly familiar.

At last Dr Squint stopped in front of a small display case. "Well, here we are," he said. "These are our wolf charms. Some very nice examples, if I do say so myself. You can take your pick." He gave Mrs Ruskin a curious look. "How long will you need it?"

"Oh, we'll be working on this project for two or three weeks," Mrs Ruskin lied. "Can you let me have it for that long?"

"Of course." Dr Squint took a tiny key and opened the case. "I have to admit, most of our visitors are not interested in these objects. But in the past, one would have had to pay a large sum to an enchanter to buy one of these. And all because of the rather primitive belief that a man can turn into a wolf. It seems a mad idea to us modern people."

"Yes, mad," Matt muttered. He could feel the fur growing on his neck. His ears were sprouting hair and his teeth were getting pointier.

"So, which one would you like?" Dr Squint asked.

"That one," said Lisa. She pointed to the ugliest charm of all. It was a tiny gold wolf's head with a horrid snarl.

When Dr Squint took the charm from the case, Matt flinched back. His whole body felt hot, as if he were a glowing coal.

Dr Squint put the charm into Mrs Ruskin's hand.

"Interesting," she said. "Really very impressive."

Matt took another step back.

"What's wrong with you?" Lisa asked.

"Nothing," Matt growled.

Dr Squint looked at Matt in surprise. "You have quite an unusual voice, young man."

"He breathed in some fumes," said Lisa. "During a Chemistry lesson." Lisa really was the best at making up excuses.

"That could be dangerous," Dr Squint said. "Is that why his eyes are so yellow?"

"Yep," Matt mumbled.

Mrs Ruskin shot Matt a worried look. She put the charm in her handbag and nodded to Matt and Lisa. "Dear Balty," she said, "thank you very much for your help. But I hope you will excuse us now. I have to get these two home."

"Oh, don't mention it," said Dr Squint, as he locked the case again. "I'm always glad to help. Come and see our demon masks sometime."

Then Dr Squint leaned down to whisper to Mrs Ruskin. "That boy really should see a doctor …"

7. BAD LUCK

Outside, the city had grown even darker. A fine rain had begun to fall and the headlights of the passing cars glistened on the wet tarmac.

Matt lifted his head and sniffed. The rain smelled good. He stuck out his tongue and caught a few drops.

Mrs Ruskin looked down at him and let out a sharp squeal. "Goodness! Matt, you really do look like a little wolf. Where is the charm?" She pulled it out of her bag and Matt jumped back towards the museum door.

"It's hot!" he said in a rough voice.

"Hot?" Mrs Ruskin rubbed the charm between her fingers. "No, it's not. But … well. Maybe we should go back to my car first. Everybody can see us up here." Her face was strained as she looked around. "Matt, you had best put up your hood. And pull it down over your face, OK?"

Matt nodded. His heart was racing and it only calmed down once the charm had vanished back into Mrs Ruskin's bag.

They ran down the stairs. Matt took three steps at a time.

"What about Mr Foulweather?" Lisa asked. "Can you smell him?"

Matt sniffed, but all he could smell was the hotdog stand at the bottom of the stairs. That smell overpowered everything else.

"I need sausages!" he said. "At least four."

"But you can't have any," Lisa said. "You know what the book said. No meat." She pulled him away by the sleeve.

Matt growled and even bared his teeth a little.

"Oh, dear me!" said Mrs Ruskin. "If you do that one more time, Matt, we'll put you on a lead. Come on, we have to cross the road. My car is over there." She peered up at the sky. "Why, for goodness sake, did it have to get dark so early, today of all days?"

It took for ever to cross the street. When at last they reached the other side Matt was dizzy from noise and hunger. He sneaked his hand into his jacket pocket and popped something into his mouth.

"Hey!" Lisa cried. "What have you got there?" She grabbed his hand and reached into his pocket. "Dog biscuits!" she squealed. "Now you've really lost it. You're eating dog biscuits!"

"So what?" Matt glared at Lisa with his yellow eyes. "I'm hungry. I'm sick with hunger. And you won't even get me sausages! Would you rather I ate that sausage dog over there?"

Lisa and Mrs Ruskin exchanged a worried look.

"Red alert!" said Lisa. "How far to your car?"

Mrs Ruskin shook her head. "The next side street."

They dragged Matt through the crowds pouring out of the shops. The jumble of smells was unbearable. Matt held his nose – which now felt quite furry.

"Pull your hood down!" Lisa hissed at him. "And look down at the pavement. Your eyes are as bright as headlights."

Matt obeyed. All these people drove him mad. He wanted to run, faster and faster and further and further away, until he could breathe again. At last Mrs Ruskin pulled them into a small side street. At last they were alone.

"Over there." Mrs Ruskin sighed with relief. "On the corner, that's my car."

"You left the lights on," Lisa said.

"So I did!" said Mrs Ruskin. "What a pain."

Mrs Ruskin unlocked the car and squeezed in behind the wheel. "It won't start!" she cried.

Matt looked up at the sky. The clouds had parted and there it was – the moon. Its blinding bright light shone straight at him.

Matt put his head back and howled.

"Oh dear ... oh goodness!" Mrs Ruskin cried. "Never, ever do that again, do you hear? That just froze the blood in my veins."

Matt didn't answer. He sniffed, sucking in the cold air. "I can smell him again," he said. "Mr Foulweather. He must be close."

"Just what we need!" Mrs Ruskin groaned. "Fine. Fine! Just keep calm … My car won't start and I'm standing in the moonlight with a little werewolf … But never mind." She drummed her fingers on the steering wheel. "I think I shall call a taxi. Yes. That's what I'll do. Where's my phone?" Mrs Ruskin got out of the car and began to rummage in her handbag. "You just sit in the car," she said.

Lisa grabbed Matt and shoved him onto the back seat. Then she got in after him. "Take that hood off!" she said.

Matt didn't want to, but he pushed it back.

"Oh my!" Lisa said. She held out her hand and stroked Matt's hairy nose. "Now you really do look like a wolf. But you feel like a fluffy guinea pig."

Matt pushed her hand away. Then he stuffed some more dog biscuits into his mouth.

Lisa shook her head. "Enjoy your meal," she said. "Have you thought of what you're going to tell your parents?"

Matt just moaned.

"Well." Mrs Ruskin dropped into the driver's seat. "The taxi will be here any minute." She passed the charm to Lisa. "Put this around his neck," she said. "He already looks too much like a wolf for my liking. No taxi in the world will take him." She sneezed. "Those eyes ... Matt, those eyes really make my skin crawl."

Lisa held the charm out to Matt. It shone in the darkness, just like his eyes.

"I don't want it!" Matt said. It came out like a bark. "I don't want that thing. It's hot."

"Put it on!" Lisa begged him. "Do you think I want a wolf on a lead as my friend from now on?"

"I don't want it!" Matt screamed. "It burns. It burns my fur!" He bared his teeth. They were as sharp as needles. The eye-teeth had grown so long that they stuck out over his lower lip.

Lisa dropped the charm in fright.

Matt pushed the door open and jumped out onto the wet street.

"I don't want it!" he screamed again.

The moonlight painted his shadow on the tarmac. A wolf's shadow, crouched, with its nose to the wind and its furry ears pricked up.

The street was deserted, but Matt could smell something. Crisps, cigarettes and smelly socks.

Foulweather.

Matt spun round.

A light flared in a dark alley – a bright light that pierced Matt's eyes. Once, twice, three times.

"At last!" Foulweather cried. "A real werewolf! And I got a picture!"

Foulweather hopped around like a toad in triumph.

Matt's whole body was shaking. He could feel the wolf inside him get angry – wild and angry. The wolf wanted to bite. The wolf wanted to hunt.

"Leave him alone!" Lisa screamed.

And Matt turned away. Away from Foulweather, away from Lisa and Mrs Ruskin. He vanished into the darkness.

8. THE WOLF

Matt ran through the dark streets, trying to get away from people. Dogs howled as he passed. Cats hissed and jumped away. The few people he passed looked after him in confusion.

Matt ran without getting tired. His legs felt as light as feathers and the cold air tasted great. The streets grew darker and emptier, but Matt ran on until all he could see around him was trees.

When at last he stopped, he found himself in a small park. Old benches stood along narrow paths. The moon shone through the branches of the trees. Matt pushed his hood back and gobbled up the last of the dog biscuits.

His stomach was still rumbling, but he tried to ignore it. He left the path and ran across a misty lawn. Then he threw his head back and howled at the moon. It sounded eerie and beautiful. A few dogs answered him from a distance. Birds flew from the trees and fluttered away, their black wings melting into the night sky.

Then Matt dropped on the wet grass, closed his eyes and tried to think. He waited for his heart to slow down. But his nose was alert and his ears were pricked. He could hear birds calling in the trees and furry paws rustling in the grass. The air smelled of rabbits.

Rabbits! Matt's stomach rumbled. His whole body grew tense and there was nothing he could do about it. He jumped up, sniffed and listened. The whole world was reduced to smells and sounds. Then, without a sound, he ran off towards the sound of tiny rustling paws.

The rabbit took fright and hopped away. It fled into the bushes, under the thorny branches and stinging nettles. Matt hunched down and followed it. His heart was racing. The nettles whipped his face and the thorns tore at his clothes, but his fur protected him. The rabbit was fast, but Matt was faster. With one last leap he jumped on top of the small animal, grabbed its hind legs and bared his fangs. The rabbit squealed like a newborn baby. It stared at Matt, eyes wide with fear.

And Matt let go.

The rabbit flew off and Matt sat among the thorns and nettles and shivered. There was rabbit fur stuck to his claws.

Then Matt got to his feet. His jacket and trousers were covered in leaves and there were even leaves stuck to his face. He tried to wipe them off with his paws, but it wasn't easy without fingers.

All of a sudden, he felt terribly tired. He struggled out of the brambles, pulled down his hood and trotted back onto the lawn. He was freezing, despite his fur. And he wanted to go home, despite the fact he had no idea what he was going to tell his parents. He didn't know where he was, but at least the wolf inside him could find the way.

Nothing was too dark for the wolf's eyes, but Matt still felt the way any 13-year-old boy feels when he walks all alone through dark streets. Only once did he growl and bare his teeth, when a man stepped into his path and stretched out his hand. The man hurried to cross the street and there it was again, for a short moment – that wonderful wolf feeling. But Matt still had the rabbit's squeals in his ears, and he was scared of himself.

When at last Matt got back to his house he didn't know what to do. No way could he show himself to his parents in this state. He unlocked the front door and crept up the stairs. Luckily the staircase was deserted.

The hideout in the attic was the only place Matt could go. The only place he could feel safe.

He crawled through the wardrobe and curled up on the old sofa. But even here Matt couldn't hide from the moon. The pale light fell through the skylight onto the worn old carpet.

'It doesn't matter,' Matt thought. He wrapped his arms around his legs. 'At least there's nobody for me to eat here, and Foulweather won't find me to take any more photos.'

Matt had no idea how long he'd been sitting there, but after what felt like hours he heard a rustle in the wardrobe and Lisa came in.

"Here you are!" she said. "Have you any idea how hard we've been looking for you? We even went to the animal shelter. Some dog-catcher could have got you."

Lisa sat down next to Matt and put an arm around him. "You don't have to worry about Mr Foulweather and his photos," she said. "They're gone. The photos, I mean. Mrs Ruskin charged at him like a dragon and snatched the camera from his hand. She pulled out the memory card and threw it into the gutter. She yelled so loud that people started poking their heads out of their windows – 'Leave the boy alone, you scoundrel!' And then she said, so low that only he and I could hear, 'You know what, Buttonbrain? I will report you to the head teacher. That's what I will do.' Foulweather just stood there as if he'd been struck by lightning. Then the taxi came and we drove all over the city, trying to find you. It must have cost Mrs Ruskin a fortune."

"I'm sorry," Matt mumbled. He looked up at the moon.

"I told your parents that you're sleeping at my house tonight," Lisa said. "OK?"

Matt nodded. He looked at his claws. "I nearly killed a rabbit tonight."

"Where?"

"In a park."

For a moment, Lisa was very quiet. Then she said, "You were hungry. And wolves can't go to the supermarket. Do you want a cheese sandwich? I have one left."

Matt shook his head. "Don't you get it? I nearly killed it! I nearly killed it and ate it – fur and bones and all."

"So what?" said Lisa. "We all eat animals all the time."

"That's different!" Matt shouted. "I didn't kill those animals."

"That's right. Somebody else had to do that for you," Lisa said. "Wolves do it themselves. That's no worse." She took out her cheese sandwich and started chewing. "Yuck! It's all dried out!"

Matt stuck his head between his knees. "You really don't get it!" he said. "It was horrible, you know? I enjoyed hunting it. That was the worst thing. And then I grabbed it by its little legs and it started screaming like a baby. And then I let it go." He looked at Lisa. "I want that charm."

"Good!" Lisa pulled the charm from her pocket.

Matt felt the heat again, but it wasn't as bad as in the museum. He looked up at the skylight. The moon had vanished. Maybe that was why the heat wasn't so bad.

Lisa put the charm into Matt's paw. It felt warm – very warm – but it didn't burn him.

Matt put it around his neck and tucked it under his jumper.

"Well?" Lisa asked. She sounded tense. "What does it feel like?"

"Like a hot potato," said Matt. "But it's OK." He yawned. "I think I'll lie down here on the sofa. We have school tomorrow."

Lisa got up. "You do that," she said. "But promise me you won't go out again. Or shall I lock the wardrobe?"

"No need," Matt mumbled. Then he fell asleep.

9. STUBBLE AND SUNGLASSES

The next morning Matt's father gave him a telling-off.

"Next time you want to sleep somewhere else, you arrange it with us first. OK?"

"OK," said Matt, as he bit into his third jam sandwich.

"What do you want on your sandwich for school?" his mother asked. "Salami?"

Matt shook his head. "I don't eat salami."

"Since when?" said Paul.

"Since today," Matt replied grouchily. "And I don't eat meat any more either."

"Who gave you that idea? One of your teachers?" his father asked. "Maybe that weird Biology teacher?"

"Definitely not him." Matt started on his fourth jam sandwich.

His mother just shook her head.

"Maybe it's something to do with those sunglasses," Paul joked. "Maybe you stop eating meat when you start wearing sunglasses at the breakfast table."

"No," said Matt. "My eyes just hurt."

And zap! His brother pulled the sunglasses off his nose.

"Matt!" his mother screamed. "You still have those yellow eyes!"

"And his stubble hasn't got any less either," his brother said. "I never heard of stubble on anyone's forehead."

"OK, I admit it." Matt put the sunglasses back on. "I took a sip of dad's baldness cure."

"You did what?" His dad nearly spilled his coffee on his tie.

"It smells so good," said Matt. He wasn't a very talented liar, but the sunglasses made it easier.

"We're going to the doctor!" his mother said. "Right after school. Maybe they'll have to pump your stomach or something!"

"It's a bit late for that," said Paul. "At least the stuff worked better on him than on dad!"

Matt's father put his hand to his bald head. "You're right," he grumbled.

Matt got up. "I've got to go," he said. "And tonight I want to sleep at Lisa's again. We're working on something for school."

"At night?" Paul asked, with a stupid grin.

"Aren't you two getting a bit too old to be sleeping at each other's houses?" his mother asked. Her face went bright red.

Matt shook his head. "You guys have funny ideas sometimes," he said. "Typical grown-ups. I've packed my toothbrush already." He walked out and slammed the door behind him.

Mr Foulweather was off sick. That was his story, at least. So Matt only had to get through four periods – double History and double Maths. History was with Mrs Ruskin, who was over the moon to see Matt alive and well – and with the charm around his neck. And he survived Maths as well. He just couldn't form a single sensible thought all day. He was afraid of the night to come. Badly afraid, although he didn't know exactly what he was afraid of. Was it the thought of turning into a wolf for ever? Or the thought that the wolf might disappear for ever? Matt wasn't sure.

He was sure that he was happy to be sitting next to Lisa. The other boys always made fun of him for being the only boy who sat next to a girl. But at least Lisa left him alone, unlike the others. 'Matt, what's with the sunglasses?' 'Matt, when did you stop shaving?' 'Hey, Matt, why's your hand all furry?'

Matt's answer was always the same. "Isn't it obvious? I'm a werewolf."

The others laughed themselves silly at his excellent joke. They did wonder why Matt suddenly ran faster than anyone else in the class – he'd always been a nobody at sports. But even that didn't make them too curious. They didn't know what to expect from a boy who volunteered to sit next to a girl – and a girl who was a head taller than him at that.

"I'll stay in the hideout tonight," Matt whispered to Lisa while Mrs Ruskin was telling them something about Alexander the Great.

"Mrs Ruskin promised she'd keep an eye on Foulweather tonight," Lisa whispered back.

Matt nodded – that was a comfort. He felt for the charm under his jumper. It had been quite cool since sunrise – but of course the wolf part of him slept during daylight.

Matt would have loved to sleep. He was so tired that he could have just put his head down on the desk and drifted off.

After class Mrs Ruskin waved them both over.

"I've spoken to the head teacher," she said in a whisper. "I told him Mr Foulweather is obsessed with the idea that a student has turned into a werewolf and has even begun to follow the student around. I think our dear Mr Foulweather may have to go and speak to a counsellor."

"Well, he'd better keep his mouth shut about werewolves there," Lisa said with a grin.

"And you?" Mrs Ruskin looked down at Matt with concern. "How are you feeling? What have you been up to all night?"

"You know ..." Matt shrugged. "Just doing wolf stuff."

Lisa giggled. "He hunted a rabbit. But he didn't eat it."

Matt gave her an angry look. "That wasn't funny," he growled. "Not funny at all."

He spun round and stormed out into the corridor. Lisa ran after him, but Matt didn't stop. He pushed and shoved his way to the stairs, flew down them at full tilt and ran out into the playground.

So Lisa didn't get it either. AT ALL. Nobody understood the way he felt. He aimed an angry kick at an empty drink can. It was one just like it that had got him into all this trouble in the first place.

"Hey, Matt!" Somebody pulled him by the sleeve.

Matt jerked his arm free. Behind him stood Batterby and Ramsay, the two nastiest kids in his year. Sadly they were also the two strongest kids in his year.

Batterby broke into a stupid grin and shoved Matt in the chest. "What's that you've got under your jumper, loser?" He yanked out the charm. "Wow! That's *ugly*."

All of a sudden Matt's chest felt very cold. The wolf woke up. He was still groggy, but he was awake.

"You look so stupid running around in sunglasses, loser," said Ramsay.

"You look so stupid running around with a head," Matt retorted. His voice sounded as rough as it had on the first night.

The two bullies were surprised. They didn't expect 'losers' to have spirit.

"You're asking for a slap," said Batterby.

"Right!" growled Ramsay.

But Matt just shook his head. "Not today," he said. Then he took off his sunglasses.

Batterby let go of Matt's jumper in alarm. He took three steps back. "Man, your eyes don't look right!"

"No?" Matt bared his teeth. A growl rose from his chest, deep and wild.

Ramsay jumped in. "Listen, there's no problem here!" he gabbled. "OK? Your sunglasses are cool! Really!"

Then Ramsay grabbed Batterby by the arm and dragged him away from the monster with the yellow eyes.

"Everything all right?" Lisa asked from behind Matt.

Matt turned around. "Yep. Everything's fine." He put his sunglasses back on and tucked the charm under his jumper again. "I didn't bite them, if that's what you're worried about."

"Might have done them some good," Lisa said.

"But maybe they would have turned into wolves too," said Matt. "And they might not stop at hunting rabbits."

Lisa shuddered. "Sorry I told Mrs Ruskin the thing about the rabbit."

"That's OK."

Batterby and Ramsay stood in the far corner of the playground and stared at them suspiciously.

"I think I'm going to miss the wolf," Matt said quietly. "It won't be easy to go back to being a weak little coward again."

"Coward?" Lisa repeated. "You've never been a coward!"

Matt shrugged. "Doesn't matter anyway. Tonight we get rid of the wolf. Even if he was a good friend sometimes."

10. FULL MOON

Night came too soon.

Matt had worn the charm all day long, but still the wolf stirred as soon as darkness fell.

He and Lisa were playing cards in their hideout at dusk. Lisa lit a few candles and when she turned around, Matt was holding his cards in paws, not hands. His fur was thicker and longer than it had been the night before.

And now he felt even more restless, even more ready to run.

Ready to hunt. Needing to hunt.

Matt rammed his claws into a piece of chocolate and put it in his mouth. It tasted awful.

Lisa looked up at the skylight. "The moon is back," she said.

"I know," Matt growled. "I can feel it. I don't even have to look." He shifted on the sofa.

"Shall we keep playing?" Lisa asked.

Matt shook his head. He threw the cards on the table and leapt up. He started to pace the room. Back and forth, up and down.

"It's not helping, is it?" Lisa sounded worried. "The charm, I mean."

Matt shrugged. "I have no idea how I'd feel without it."

"Well, at least you're not walking on all fours yet," Lisa said. It was clear she wanted to laugh, but the laughter had stuck in her throat. Matt knew he looked too miserable.

"I have to go down for dinner," Lisa said. "But I'll sneak back up here right after, OK?"

Matt just nodded.

Lisa crawled into the wardrobe and Matt heard her lock the door. He looked around. There really was no way out of here. Boxes and old furniture were piled up to the ceiling. Matt lowered his shaggy head and started to pace again. Up and down, faster and faster, until at last he was running. He jumped up on the wardrobe and tore open the boxes with his claws. The charm on his chest was getting warmer, but the wolf was growing wilder.

Where was Lisa?

Matt swiped out the candles with his paw. Then he pushed a box under the skylight and opened the small hatch. He sucked in a huge breath of cold night air. He held out a paw and it turned silver in the moonlight. Now the charm was getting hot – very hot. It was burning his fur. Matt tore it from his neck and threw it down on the carpet. Then he pulled himself through the hatch and jumped out onto the roof.

Now all that was above him was the moon and the stars. Matt sat on the roof and howled. He howled until the cold night air hurt his throat. Then he pulled off his jumper and threw it away. He watched in wonder as it drifted towards the ground, where tiny cars crawled through the night like little glowing insects. Then Matt heard a noise behind him and a scent that he knew crept up his nose.

"Matt? Come down from there, now!"

Lisa was back. Her head poked through the hatch. She looked at him in horror.

"I heard you howl," she said. "And then I found this!" She held up the charm.

Matt bared his fangs. "It was burning my fur," he growled. Then he pricked his ears. Two birds were flying above him. He licked his lips.

"So, what now?" Lisa asked. "Are you going to sit up there until a crow flies into your mouth? Or until the fire brigade gets you down? Mrs Brewer is already out in the hall."

Matt crouched down and stared at Lisa with his yellow eyes for a long while.

"I'm going to put the charm on you again," Lisa told him. "And if I fall off the roof doing it, it'll be your fault."

Lisa pushed herself through the hatch, put one foot on the roof and then pulled herself up to the ridge. The charm was dangling from her wrist on its cord.

Matt growled. His white fangs were bared again and he was shaking as he crawled away from her on all fours, like a dog. Or like a wolf. The ridge of the roof was no wider than one of his paws.

Lisa swung one leg over the ridge. She didn't look down. She squeezed her legs against the cold tiles.

"I am not afraid of you," she told Matt. "No matter how much you show me your fangs. Even wolves don't eat their friends. I am going to put this charm round your neck, because I don't want to sit next to a wolf in school. I can't play cards with a wolf, or annoy his big brother. Or go to the cinema and see stupid films. Now, put your head down before I fall off this awful roof."

She shuffled closer and closer to Matt.

Matt didn't move.

Lisa reached out and hung the charm around his neck.

It burned. It burned like fire!

"No!" Matt screamed. "Take it off!"

He leapt to his feet and swayed on the ridge as he pulled at the charm.

"Be careful!" Lisa screamed. She tried to hold on to his legs, but Matt kicked her away. He tore the cord with his claws and the charm slipped down the roof and vanished into the darkness.

"Oh no!" Lisa moaned. She looked at Matt with tears in her eyes.

"How could you do that?" she yelled. "What's going to protect you now?" She pressed her hands to her face and sobbed. "Now you're going to be a wolf for ever. There'll be nothing left of Matt any more – nothing!"

Matt stood and looked down at her. The moon painted his big hairy shadow on the roof.

"I couldn't help it," he whispered. "I couldn't, Lisa."

He shivered as he crouched down on the ridge. He waited for what Lisa had said would happen – for Matt to vanish and for only a wolf to be left. A wolf that might not even remember who Lisa was.

And then a dark veil fell over his eyes. He looked up at the moon, confused. The moon was as bright as ever, but the night sky was dark. Pitch black, as Matt hadn't seen it for days.

"Lisa!" he whispered. "It's dark again."

"What are you talking about?" Lisa was still holding her hands in front of her face. "Of course it's dark. It's the middle of the night."

"No, you don't understand!" Matt yelled. "It's never really dark for wolves."

Lisa took her hands from her face and looked at Matt. She stroked his cheek with an expression of wonder. "Your fur is vanishing!" she whispered. "How is that possible?"

Matt lifted his hands and saw that Lisa was right. The fur was all gone, as if it had been wiped away. Matt shivered as he rubbed his bare arms. It was terribly cold up here on the roof without fur.

"What about your hearing and sense of smell?" Lisa asked.

Matt sucked in the night air. "I can still smell like a wolf," he said. "And hear like one, too."

"But you don't look like a wolf any more!" Lisa exclaimed. "How ...?" She stopped in the middle of her question, leaned forward and

CORNELIA FUNKE

pointed at Matt's chest. The fur was gone from there too, except for a little fluff. But where the charm had hung, there was now the imprint of a snarling wolf.

"It did help!" Lisa whispered. Then she laughed.

"What helped?" Matt asked. He squinted down at his chest, but he couldn't see anything in the dark.

"The charm. It branded your skin!" Lisa took Matt's finger and put in on the place on his chest. The skin felt very warm.

"You mean it's like a tattoo?" Matt asked.

"Yes. That's why you didn't change. You're wolf-proof now."

Matt stroked the small mark. "But he's still there," he whispered.

Lisa frowned. "The wolf?"

Matt nodded. He could feel him. Deep inside. Not quite so hungry and a little sleepy, but definitely still there. Matt felt his teeth with his tongue. They were human teeth again, only a tiny bit more pointy.

"I think you're right." Lisa leaned forward and looked in his eyes. "Your eyes aren't yellow any more, but they're still … different."

"It doesn't matter." Matt jumped up and balanced on his bare feet on the roof ridge. "I feel great!" he yelled. "Wolf-ishly great and I don't have a craving for guinea pigs any more!"

Then Matt threw his head back and howled at the moon. It didn't sound quite as rough and wild as it had just an hour before, but it still felt good.

Our books are tested
for children and young people by
children and young people.

Thanks to everyone who consulted on
a manuscript for their time and effort in
helping us to make our books better
for our readers.